What a Story!

By kids for kids

Hi there, it's your favorite author, AJ Hard. As you can tell by now, this is not a *Shiver and Fears* book. It's not a *Magical Times* book either.

In this book, I'm not the author. Instead, I'm the publisher. This book holds 4 interesting stories made by 3rd graders... well at this point they're not 3rd graders any more.

However, they created some interested tales during the contest "What's Your Story". Have you heard of my latest book "Terror Tales 2"? No? You should, it features 8 kids who created their own story titles as I wrote them.

But this time, these titles were not just created by kids, they were written by kids too.

Story tellers come in many different sizes and ages.

Anyone can be a storyteller; they aren't always perfect, but they have a way of being creative.

Our first story comes from Aaliyah she made a scary story about a box that can whisper, and apparently it flies too. Before I tell you these stories, let me tell you how this book will work. First, you will see the raw material put together by the mind of a child. That way you can see how a child thinks when writing.

Then, I will show you my input on the story. It might turn out to be different than what you read from the child's mind. I'll explain why.

Lastly, I'll put my thoughts into the story. Hey! Maybe it'll get you thinking too! Isn't that why reading is so interesting? Because we all have different visions on how things look in a book.

Let's start, shall we?

the Whispering Box

it was a girl walking and a Boy
with a box not JUSt A
Box But (it) can whisper
and the B@X can
fly and it got on her
head and she was flying
and they took her to
a place it was call a
secret room and the Boys
name is elijah and the
girls name is Princessand
the lock her in a room

with the whispering box
and the whispering box
Scared her to much.
She pass away in 1929 and
the whispering box
made the boy run away
for a long time but the
boy came back it was someon
up to no good so the
whispering box made the boy
pass away in 2007 so
princess was not died she

was sleep till 2007 the

time Elijah was died

and they let the

girl sold live her lire she istt you

and he was 25

so they killed and he is com

-ing for you look out for

him mahahahaha. waoth

out for him

Now, here is my version of
the same story...

The Whispering Box

There was an 11- year-old girl named Princess and a 25-year-old man named Elijah.

Elijah had a box, but no ordinary box. It was a whispering box that could fly.

One day in the year 1929, Princess was taking a walk. Meanwhile, Elijah was up to no good.

He used the box to place on Princess' head. It made her

fly all the way to a place
called The Secret Room.

Princess was then trapped
in the room with the box.
Princess was scared.

Princess soon passed away.
Once Elijah knew she was
gone, the whispering box
told him to run away for
years.

In the year 2007, Elijah
returned with the whispering
box. Princess had returned
too, for she was not dead but

had been asleep the whole time.

Princess then used the whispering box to make Elijah pass away. Princess then was able to live her life. But, Elijah might be back. So watch out! Because he's coming for you!

When I first read this story, my thoughts were very different. First of all, I thought Princess and Elijah were friends. It never said so, but for them to both know about this box made it seem like they were sharing.

Another thing I learned after reading this story was the box is evil! It sounded as though Princess found this box and took it for adventures.

You know what, maybe she did. Maybe Elijah took it from her and because he used it for evil purposes, she became afraid of it. I ask you read the raw material again.

Pay attention to what details of left behind. Maybe you'll image the story different from what I did. I do enjoy it. Here's why: Most authors put so much work into the details that readers begin to miss the point of the story entirely.

When Aaliyah wrote her story she made sure the story was told. Now, the details were put in, just at a later time. This shows that the plot was focused more than the details.

Because of this, the story has a some-what free vision of the characters and the scenery. Nice job Aaliyah. Keep working, and you'll grow to an amazing writer someday!

Next we have the writer of The Whispering Monster. This story was put together by a young boy, Alonzo.

He wrote his story, however, alone it lacks detail. This young boy needed a little assistance. So I helped his story a little. You will see his raw material and a piece of work we did together.

Wisping
Mocster
Alonzo
Porter

A Writn
By Alonzo Porter

this is wisping

I Met a Boy name Alrizo.
He Love to wisping.

He Love Wisping
He Met a frien
Name, Jack Day
Love to Wisping
cAn we Play
footBoll Day
Wisping in Play
a Boy name squek
He Love to Play
footBoll.
the enD

Love
to Wisping
Byilly

Hmmm...
Let's look at
this again.

Plot

Name _______________

Throw the ball
Larenzo bathroom
Jack got hurt (ankle)
Person Squeaks ~~tries~~ calls for LaRenzo

La Renzo - asked
Jack Day - friend (monitor)

setting

field day

LaRenzo helps using a kit
on a bench
Jack was left on the bench
went home for hot cholocate

solution

Alonzo Porter

be a little hard, this might
help...

Now for the results:

The Whispering Monster

There once was a boy named Lorenzo. He liked to whisper. He also liked to play football.

One day on the football field, Lorenzo met a monster. His name was Jack Day.

Lorenzo asked Jack if he
wanted to play football.
Jack said yes.

While they were playing,
they met another kid
named Squeaks.

So while Lorenzo went to
the bathroom him and
Jack were playing
together. While playing
until Lorenzo got back.

Jack got his ankle hurt. Squeaks called for Lorenzo's help.

Lorenzo came back with his kit and helped him.

Jack, now on the bench, had to sit out while the others continued their game of football.

Later, it was time to head home. They all went to Lorenzo's house and all

enjoyed a cup of hot
chocolate.

What I really liked about this story is how it's a different look on monsters. I mean there are multiple stories with monster who are friends with people. But this one wasn't really about the monsters. It was about problem a monster had.

Now, reading it I barely understood the process. There a whispering monster, they played football... but there's more going on in the story, right?

I had to get with Alonzo and find out. So, for those of you who might want to write a story and have no clue how, it's your lucky day. Because he's a clue on how: Use the SPS scale.

Let me explain, we all know a story has a

beginning, middle, and end. Well, when we break it up we learn the beginning always starts off with the setting. Who is involved in the story, where were they when it happened, and what's the scenery.

After you explain all that, then you get to the middle; the plot. That's where you grow into the problem. Once you get deep enough into the problem, then you hit the end: the solution to the problem.

Once that was settled with Alonzo, the story just needed to be put together.

Now, I know with this story I did some work, but if I hadn't do you think this story would make sense?

Keep writing Alonzo,
practice makes perfect!

Now, these next two stories did need help. But the ideas was theirs. Now although some kids can write what's on their minds, others can't express it on paper. So with a little help these stories were made with my assistance.

Here is the Dayan story. This is his story idea:

(School)

Character: Dayon   litte nieghbor

little nieghbor ~~is~~ ~~bully~~ annoying

alway around

call ~~dad~~ (dad)

call
dad
talk and tell the rules

Hmm... not much to go with. But as an author, you just put the story together the best way you can. Here is Dayan's story: The Little Neighbor.

The Little Neighbor

One day a boy named Dayan lived next door to a very small kid. He was mostly known as the little neighbor.

Dayan didn't like the little neighbor because he was always bothering him in school. The little neighbor would always talk to Dayan.

While Dayan was listening to the teacher, the little neighbor would distract him.

Dayan tried talking to his teacher about his problem, but it didn't help.

Dayan came up with an idea. He asked his dad to call Grandpa to talk to the little neighbor.

When Grandpa came by, Dayan asked if he had any

solutions to his problem.
Grandpa did.

Grandpa walked over to
the little neighbor's house.
He explained to the little
boy that his grandson
didn't like his behavior.

The little neighbor walked
back over to Dayan and
told him how sorry he was
for bothering him.

Dayan was now happy that
the little neighbor
wouldn't bother him again.

Now I will admit, this story isn't the greatest in the world. But, it is a start. In fact, this is the perfect example of how stories are created.

Some stories are fictional based on actually events. When Dayan made this story, it was obviously made by an experience in his life. How did it end up? Not sure, but this story

states that Dayan's dad
told his dad to solve the
problem.

...I'm not making this up!
He really told me his
grandfather solved the
whole problem by just
talking to the little
neighbor.

Is that how he solves his
real problems? Who
knows, but I'm sure he
could make some

interesting stories based
off his life.

Our last story is called The Red Picture. Although I forget the name of this story teller, but she goes by the initials of S.W.

S.W. story impressed me, because it showed how she likes to solve problems without any kind of battle.

She was actually the first person who required help. She had the words, just

didn't know how to write
it.

She was really determined
to get this story in before
the deadline. And there's
no reason to deny her try.

So this story is about
battling a disagreement,
most kids don't know how
to settle disagreements,
others know how, just
can't make a settlement.

Well this story here has a simple solution and the avoidance of conflict.

Here is the plot:

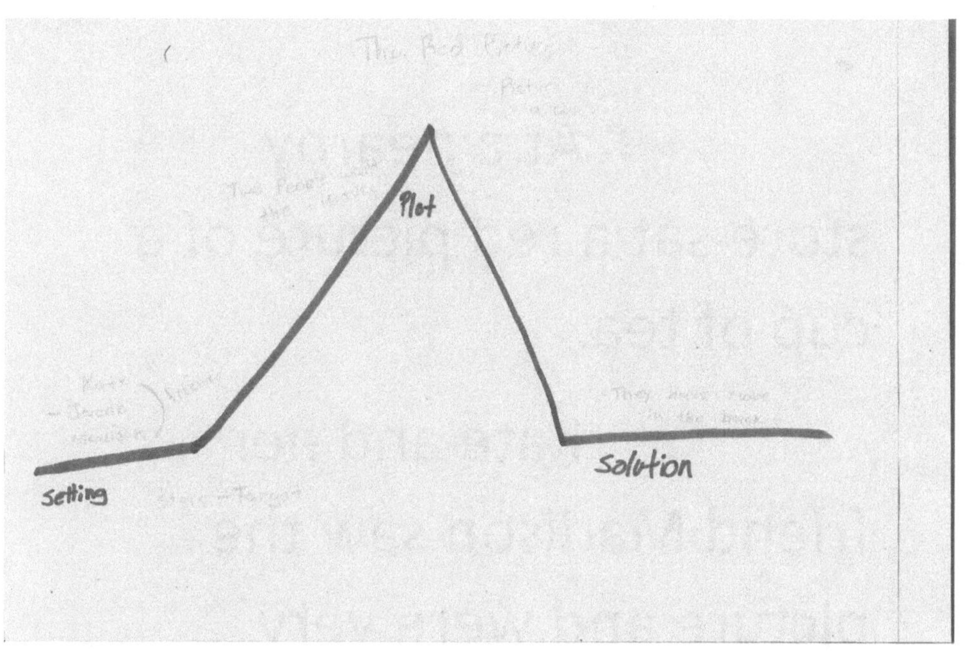

Now to introduce you to
The Red Picture:

At a nearby
store sat a red picture of a
cup of tea.

Kate and her
friend Madison saw the
picture and were very
happy. They both loved

the color red and wanted
to buy the picture.

Meanwhile,
there was another person
who wanted the picture. A
young boy named Jacob
saw the red picture too.

Jacob, nor Kate
or Madison wanted to
fight about the picture. So
they decided to talk about
it.

Madison
explained to Jacob why
they should have it. To
place in their clubhouse.

Jacob wanted it
for his bedroom.

There was no
other solution but to ask
the manager who should
have it.

The manager
explained to the kids they
could all get the red

picture. The manager took
the 3 kids to the back of
the store.

He gave the
picture of the red tea cup
to each kid. They each
bought one and took it
home.

Don't you wish
all problems could be
solved like that? Way to go
S.W.! You and the rest of
the young writers have
done amazing work.

Who knows
what other stories will be
put together by kids. They
may not all be published
like this one, but I'm sure
the stories are good.

Hey, maybe you know of a kid who has a story to tell. Who knows, I might be interested in writing it.

As for now, I'm AJ Hard. I had fun writing this, but now I'm heading back into my station and writing more Shiver and Fears stories.

I encourage you
to keep writing, in the
meantime, CHILL OUT.

Check out AJ Hard's originals at any book site;

- Shiver and Fears (series)
- Magical Times (series)
- Rainbow of Friends
- An Auto Bio: The J in AJ
- The Story Behind Easter